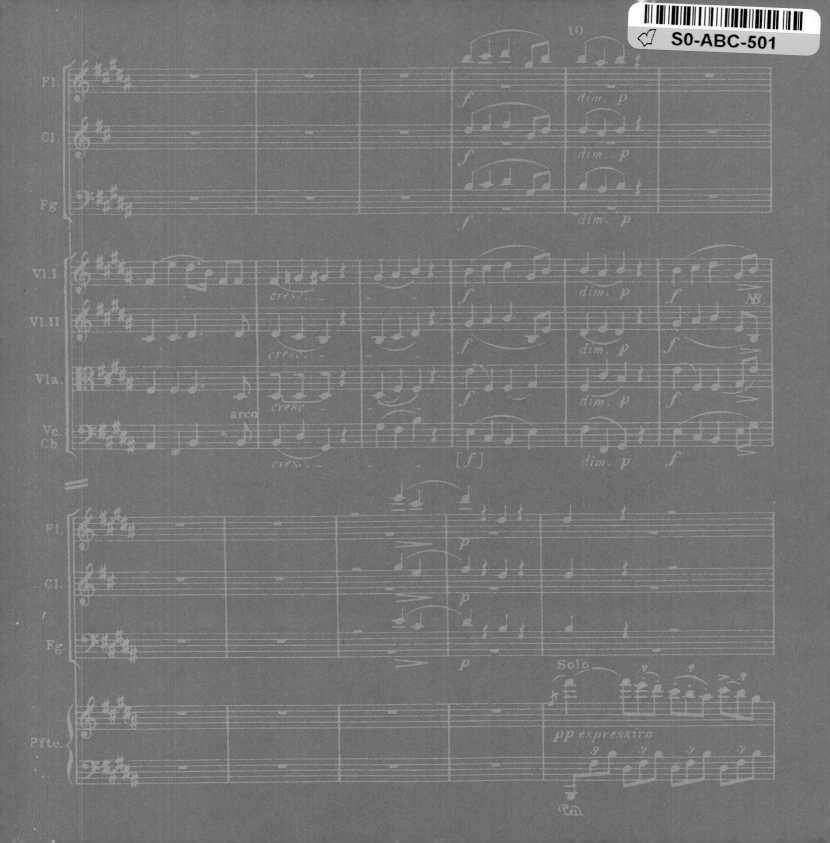

# The Living Piano

BY BARRIE CARSON TURNER

Alfred A. Knopf  New York

THIS IS A BORZOI BOOK PUBLISHED BY ALFRED A. KNOPF, INC.

Text copyright © 1996 by Macmillan Children's Books. CD Sound

Recording (MACCOM 2) copyright © 1996 by EMI Records Ltd.

Picture credits appear on page 47. All other illustrations

copyright © 1996 by Macmillan Children's Books, London.

All rights reserved under International and Pan-American Copyright

Conventions. Published in the United States by Alfred A. Knopf,

Inc., New York. Distributed by Random House Inc., New York.

Published in Great Britain by Macmillan Children's Books, a

division of Macmillan Publishers Limited, London, in 1996.

Printed in Singapore

ISBN 0-679-88180-8

10 9 8 7 6 5 4 3 2 1

# Contents

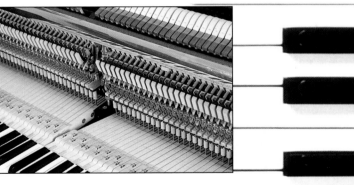

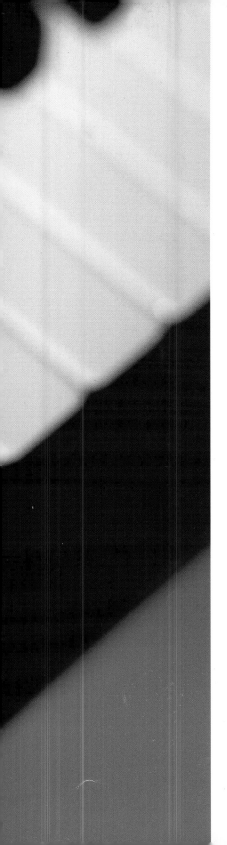

# Overture

Playing and listening to music, as well as learning about it, is one of the most popular and exciting pastimes in the world today.

It is sometimes said that the piano is the most romantic of all instruments. In the nineteenth century composers found themselves drawn to the piano, and there grew up a school of performer-composers dedicated to expressing their composing skills through the new, improved instrument.

Numerous compositions from this period have descriptive titles, like the many pieces by Schumann. By using evocative titles, composers were reflecting their belief that the piano was able to represent a whole range of thoughts and images in music.

Almost every composer to the present day has written important works for the piano. In the days of Scarlatti and Bach, the first two composers featured in this book, the piano was in its infancy, and the harpsichord was the preferred instrument. Yet within fifty years, by the time Beethoven was writing his first keyboard works, the harpsichord had become quite outdated.

The keyboard family is immensely varied and is represented by a great number of instruments other than the piano. A large church organ playing at full volume could drown out an entire orchestra, and yet the eighteenth-century spinet can hardly be heard beyond a distance of a few feet!

Modern pianos vary from the compact upright to the huge and heavy concert grand, measuring almost ten feet long and weighing nine hundred pounds. The sections on how the piano works and making pianos will give you insight into the complexities of the instrument's construction.

The audio compact disc from EMI that accompanies this book features extracts of music written by ten great composers. The short section "ON THE CD," which appears in the text for each composer, tells you a little about the music.

Whether you are already a keyboard player, just beginning lessons, or simply interested in keyboard music, *The Living Piano* will add to the range of your knowledge and understanding of the piano.

# The Keyboard Family

### Organ

The first organ was made in Greece over two thousand years ago. It was called the *hydraulis,* and it used air and water pressure, by means of a hand pump, to make the sound. In Roman times the instrument was played at ritual ceremonies and gladiatorial displays. Because of these pagan associations the organ was very slow to enter Christian worship.

### Clavichord

The strings of the clavichord (two for each note, rather than one, to increase the volume) were struck with small brass blades called "tangents." The tangent stayed against the string until the key was released, which allowed the finger to alter the intensity of the note by varying the pressure on the key. The instrument had a soft, delicate sound.

### Spinet

Like the clavichord, the spinet was a quiet instrument, more suited to home use than on the concert platform. The strings were sounded by means of a plucking mechanism. When a key was pressed, a seesaw action raised a piece of wood, called a "jack." A quill attached to the jack plucked the string, producing a pleasant, tinkly sound.

*The church organ today is the largest of all keyboard instruments, with pipes on some organs measuring almost thirty feet long.*

*Above: The clavichord dates from the fifteenth century and was the first keyboard instrument to be played regularly in the home. Because of its box shape it was small enough to be placed on a table.*

*Below: The spinet was popular as a keyboard instrument for about a hundred years, from the early days of Bach to the death of Mozart. The word "spinet" comes from the Latin word* spina, *or "thorn"– referring to the quill that plucked the string.*

## Harpsichord

For four hundred years, almost to the end of the eighteenth century, the harpsichord was the most popular of all keyboard instruments. It was a large instrument, often elaborately decorated, and had a fine, strong sound. Large harpsichords had two or even three keyboards stacked one above the other, as well as a variety of devices and mechanisms to change or enhance the tone.

*The piano is the most versatile of all the keyboard instruments. Its huge range of notes, capacity for playing louds and softs, and unique ability to blend well with other instruments make it second to none.*

*Above: In Bach's day no orchestral or chamber music piece was complete without the harpsichord. Like its smaller cousin, the spinet, the strings were plucked by quills.*

## Piano

In the early years of the nineteenth century the piano moved out of the houses of the wealthy into middle-class homes, and toward the end of the century entered the worlds of jazz and music hall. By the early years of the twentieth century the piano was a common sight in the home.

## Harmonium

In 1840 a French instrument maker designed a new instrument that worked like a mouth organ, or harmonica, but was operated from a keyboard. The harmonium created its sound by means of a series of thin metal strips called reeds, one for each note. The reeds were activated by compressed air from bellows, operated by the feet.

*The harmonium was very popular and was played in the home, as well as in churches and chapels, where it can occasionally still be heard today.*

*Above: The player carries the piano accordion by a strap around the neck, leaving both hands free to play the instrument.*

## Piano Accordion

The piano accordion is similar to the harmonium in that it, too, uses reeds as its sound source. It is cleverly constructed to sound when the bellows are being contracted or expanded. The melody is played on the tiny keyboard by the right hand, while the left hand operates the bellows and a series of buttons to produce the bass notes and accompanying chords. The instrument is a French invention and is still very much associated with the street and café music of Paris.

## Player Piano

The first mechanical piano was hand cranked and worked like a musical box. Early nineteenth-century street musicians wheeled the instrument around the streets. A system was later designed that could be placed over the keyboard of an ordinary piano, with finger-like levers playing the keys. Eventually this system was incorporated into the piano itself. The instrument used rolls of punched paper and was worked by foot-operated bellows (later by an electric motor). In 1900 the "pianola" was first marketed, and player pianos have since also been known by this name.

## Celesta

The celesta looks like a small upright piano and in fact works in the same way as a piano—but the hammers strike tuned metal bars instead of strings. The sound it produces is high and singing.

*The Hammond Organ was an immediate success, popular in churches, cinemas, and radio studios, as well as in the home.*

## Hammond Organ

The first electric keyboard was made over a hundred years ago in the U.S.A. It was called the Telharmonium, and it weighed 200 tons! In 1939 the inventor Laurens Hammond launched his "Hammond Organ," which relied on revolving steel discs spinning through electromagnetic fields to create its sound. During the 1950s smaller portable keyboards were developed, and finally, in the 1960s, with the development of the microchip, the modern organ keyboard was born.

*The celesta was patented in Paris in 1886 and is featured in several orchestral works.*

# Instrumental Groups

### Music for Solo Piano

More music has been written for the piano than for any other solo instrument. There are probably more recitals (a concert featuring one major instrument or voice) for piano than for any other instrument. Television themes, film scores, and much orchestral music has been arranged for piano on many different levels of difficulty, to add to the huge selection of piano music available today.

### Piano Duets

A duet is a piece for two performers. Because the piano has an immensely wide range of notes, duets usually only need one instrument, although some composers have written more elaborate pieces for two pianos.

### Piano Trios

A trio is for three performers, but "Piano trio" does not mean a trio for three pianos! The title usually means a work for piano, violin, and cello. Beethoven's famous *Archduke* Trio is for this combination of instruments.

### Piano Quartets

A piano quartet is for four instruments, usually piano, violin, viola, and cello, although the composer Olivier Messiaen's *Quatuor pour la fin du temps* (Quartet for the End of Time), written in 1941 when he was a prisoner of war, is for piano, violin, clarinet, and cello. This unusual choice of instruments was dictated by the musical skills of the composer's fellow prisoners.

## The Piano as an Accompanying Instrument

Unlike most other instruments, keyboard instruments have the ability to play more than one note at once (chords), which makes them ideal for accompanying other instruments. Composers have used piano accompaniments in almost every situation — to accompany solo instruments and singers, as well as large choral works.

## Piano Concertos

The word concerto was originally used rather vaguely in music, to describe a "performance together." It has come to mean a composition for, usually, one solo instrument and orchestra. Mozart was the first great composer to write concertos for the piano, including works for two and even three pianos!

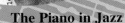

## The Piano in Jazz

The piano is an extremely popular instrument in jazz. It appears most often as a member of the jazz trio, together with drums and bass. The powerful sound of the piano is particularly suited to the strong rhythmic beat of jazz. There have been many great solo jazz pianists, such as Oscar Peterson (above), whose skills include not only an astounding piano technique but also an impressive talent for keyboard improvisation (music made up as it is being performed).

# The History of the Piano

### Cristofori's First Piano

In 1698 the Italian harpsichord maker Bartolomeo Cristofori began work on a special new keyboard instrument. His aim was to build an instrument that could play both loud and soft (unlike the popular harpsichord of the day, which could only play at one volume level). In 1709 the new instrument was finished and was called simply *gravicembalo col piano e forte*—"harpsichord with soft and loud." It later came to be known as the "pianoforte," or piano.

Cristofori faced many problems in the design of the new instrument. One problem he tackled successfully was how to prevent a hammer, having struck the string, from bouncing back and hitting the string a second time. His solution was to design a mechanism that today we call the "escapement."

In 1732 the composer Lodovico Giustini published twelve sonatas for Cristofori's piano—the first music ever written for the instrument. On the score the composer marked where the music is to be played "loud" and "soft."

*Cristofori's pianos had two strings to each note, rather than one (to make the instrument sound louder). The strings were struck with small square hammers tipped with leather. The tone of the instrument was fairly weak—which, of course, greatly pleased rival harpsichord makers.*

### Silbermann's New Model

News of Cristofori's invention spread abroad, and soon other instrument makers began building pianos. In Germany the organ builder Gottfried Silbermann excitedly demonstrated his latest piano to Bach, but the composer was not very impressed. The high notes were poor, Bach said, and the weight of the keys was too heavy, which made the instrument exhausting to play. So Silbermann redesigned his piano to make the keys lighter and easier to play, and when Bach played the new instrument, he was much more complimentary.

**The Square Piano**

The earliest pianos were "grand" pianos, large instruments with the strings stretching away from the player. They were elegant pieces of furniture in their own right, but rather cumbersome. German builders began to make smaller instruments, which they called "square" pianos. Square pianos became particularly popular in Britain when Johannes Zumpe, a pupil of Silbermann, moved to London in 1760. Zumpe's popularity as a piano maker spread far and wide, and many of his instruments were exported to France and even to America. It was the square piano and its popularity in America that brought about the next major improvement in the instrument.

*An elaborate harpsichord in Bach's house.*

***Left:*** *The strings in all square pianos run from side to side. Makers took this space-saving idea from the clavichord.*

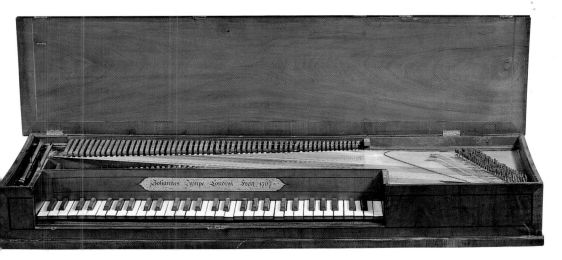

## The Iron Frame and the Sustaining Pedal

Piano strings are stretched across a harp-like structure called the "frame." In early instruments the frame was made of wood and braced with metal. But the climate in parts of America caused the wooden frame to expand and contract, which affected the strings, and the pianos frequently went out of tune. In 1825 the Boston piano maker Alpheus Babcock had the idea of casting the frame entirely in metal. A metal frame did not expand and contract as much as a wooden one, and so the tuning of the instrument remained more stable. This idea spread, and eventually all pianos were built with a metal frame. The use of an iron frame today is especially important in grand pianos, where the total tension of the strings equals many tons. An iron frame also means the strings can be thicker and tighter, which improves the tone of the instrument.

Another innovation was developed in London, which by the end of the eighteenth century had become an important center for piano making. In 1783 the British firm of Broadwood introduced what is now one of the most important features of the modern piano—the "sustaining" pedal. Eventually all pianos incorporated this improvement, and later a corresponding "soft" pedal was added. Larger instruments occasionally added a third pedal to sustain only some notes.

*The piano sent to Beethoven in 1818 as a gift from Broadwood, the London piano manufacturers.*

14

## Upright Pianos

Following the success of the square piano, makers looked for ways of achieving the sound quality of a grand piano but from a smaller instrument. Clearly the simplest way would be to place the strings and action of the grand piano on end. The result was an extremely tall instrument called a "Giraffe" piano. But this looked inelegant and awkward in a small room. In 1811 the London maker Robert Wornum came up with a more compact design, and "upright" pianos, based on this improved model, were born.

## Famous Names

The piano has come a long way since Cristofori's first instrument. Many makers, famous in their day, are now known only by the nameplate on their surviving instruments. However, three famous companies, all founded in 1853, are still very much alive today: the German firms of Bechstein and Blüthner, and the American firm of Steinway—names that are seen regularly in the best concert halls throughout the world.

## Overstringing

Another idea that enhanced the sound quality of the upright piano was developed in France. High and low strings were diagonally crossed over each other, which allowed the smaller upright piano to accommodate longer strings. Longer strings meant a more resonant (louder) instrument. Later this idea was adapted for grand pianos, and today all the best pianos are "overstrung."

15

# How the Piano Works

**Case**

**Frame**
The cast-iron frame allows the highest possible string tension, which contributes to the powerful resonance of the instrument. It also helps keep the strings in tune.

**Steel Tuning Pins**
One for each string.

**Steel Hitch Pins**
Pins at the lower end of the frame, to which the strings are fixed.

**Overstringing**
Strings set diagonally are longer and vibrate more powerfully, which means the instrument seems louder. The overstringing also helps to distribute the tension of the strings acting on the frame.

It could be argued that the piano is a stringed instrument, as much of its sound is created by vibrating strings. But in the traditional grouping of instruments the piano has always been a member of the keyboard family. The mechanics of the piano—how the keys lift the hammers to strike the strings—is called the "action." The sound of the instrument—whether round and smooth, or sharp and jerky—depends a lot on how good the action is. A good action must be responsive and, very important, the correct "weight." A heavy action will tire the player—too much effort is required to press the keys. A light action may seem easy to work with at first, but may cause the player to strike some notes accidentally. It is important that each hammer is identically weighted and at the same distance from the string—or some notes will sound more quickly than others.

The sound created by the vibrating strings is amplified by the soundboard, which acts like a diaphragm to improve the resonance of the instrument. The wooden case, or cabinet, acts like a sound box and helps swell the sound. The piano lid on the top of the case can be opened to increase the volume of sound.

**Hammers**
When a key is pressed, it causes a hammer to strike the strings.

**Dampers** cover the strings to stop any unwanted vibrations. When a key is pressed, the damper for that note is raised, and when the key is released, it falls back again.

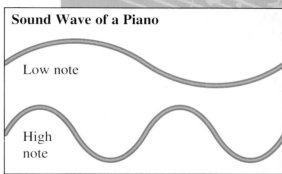

**Sound Wave of a Piano**

Low note

High note

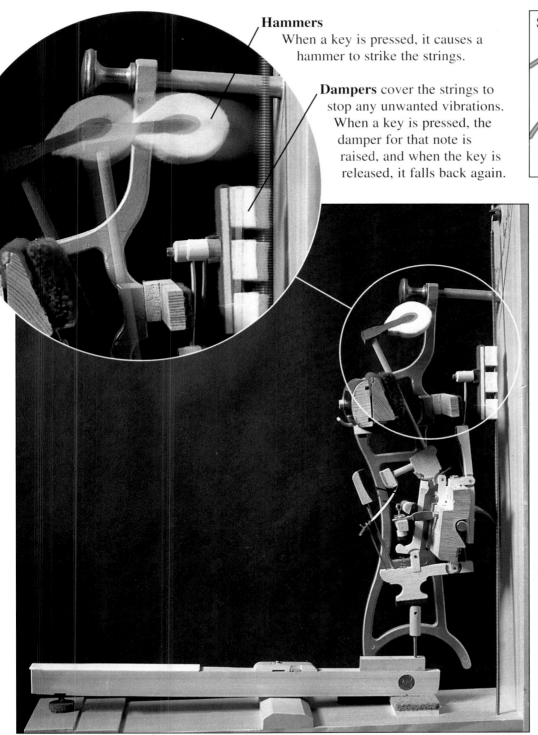

**Soft pedal (left pedal)** moves the hammers nearer the strings so that they are unable to strike as powerfully (and therefore produce a softer sound). Some soft pedals raise a piece of felt between the hammers and the strings to deaden the sound.

**Sustaining pedal (right pedal)** lifts all the dampers off the strings regardless of which keys have been pressed, and allows a note or chord to continue sounding even after it has been released by the hand.

# How the Piano Is Made

Pianos are made in a variety of styles and sizes, from the small, modern upright, suited to home use, to the concert grand. The largest individual part of the instrument is the iron frame. At the heart of the piano is the action, each part of which must work smoothly and be finely balanced.

All construction materials used in the building of the instrument must be of the highest quality if the piano is to survive many years of hard wear. It is important to have the piano tuned regularly.

The piano tuner adjusts the tension of the strings by tightening or loosening the tuning pins.

The **wooden frame** is the foundation part of the upright piano. It is usually made of oak timbers, but sometimes a combination of wood, steel, and iron is used.

The shaped **soundboard** —a slightly curved piece of spruce wood about half an inch thick—is fixed vertically in position on the frame.

The hardwood **bridges**, which bring the strings into contact with the soundboard, are glued and screwed into position.

The **pedals** are worked by a system of levers and pivots called the "trapwork."

The irregularly shaped **iron frame**, which is cast from one piece of metal, is bolted into position.

The **strings** are fixed in position, passing from the **tuning pins** over the wooden bridge to be attached again at the lower end of the iron frame to steel **hitch pins**.

The **key bed** is fitted firmly to the main framework of the instrument.

The **hammers**, which vary in size between the treble and bass strings, are made from long pieces of wood molding. Felt is wrapped around the wood under high pressure and glued to the wood. Finally, the long strip of wood and felt is cut into individual hammers.

The light, softwood **keys** are sawn from a single board of layered wood. The white notes were originally covered with ivory, and the black notes with ebony. Today, however, these natural materials have been replaced with plastic.

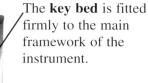

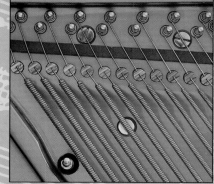

**Above: Bass strings**—one string to each note. The strings are steel, overwound with copper or brass wire. This thickens the strings while still allowing them to be flexible enough to produce a good sound.

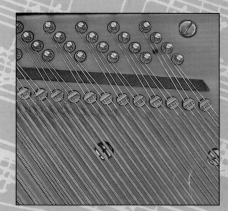

**Above: Middle strings**—two strings to each note make a louder sound.

**Below: High strings**—three strings to each note help balance the loudness of the lower strings.

# How the Piano Is Played

It is sometimes said that the piano is the most romantic of all instruments because of its ability to represent a whole range of thoughts, emotions, and images in music.

### Staccato

In piano music staccato playing means each note is separated from the next. Staccato (Italian for "detached") is possible on nearly every instrument, but is especially effective on the piano. It is used particularly for light, bouncy tunes.

### Legato

Legato means the opposite of staccato—that is, "joined": the sound of each note follows the next without any gaps. Perfect legato playing, used in songful melodies, is very beautiful on the piano.

### Playing Position

All piano teachers agree that sitting at the keyboard in an upright position is best. However, no player—beginner or advanced—remains entirely still during a performance.

## Una Corda

This Italian expression means "one string"—that is, "play with the soft pedal." Early keyboard instruments had two strings per note. The soft pedal moved the keyboard action sideways, which meant each hammer hit only one string, and made the instrument sound softer. In modern instruments the sideways action is the same, so the hammer misses one string where there are two or three (the single bass string is unaffected). Pianists use this form of expression when they want the piano to sound very thin and muted.

## Fingering

Students of the piano often find the study of fingering boring. However, in order to play the piano well, it is important to use correct fingering. Professional players know how they will finger every single note of a piece before they perform it! Good, well-organized fingering is important for smooth playing.

## Stretching an Octave

Octaves, especially for the left hand, used to add power to the bass line, are commonplace in piano music. Many young players with small hands find playing octaves difficult at first. However, as the hands grow, stretching an octave becomes no problem.

## Playing a Chord

Beginner pianists soon progress from playing single notes in each hand to playing chords. Chords appear more often in the left hand, as this hand usually acts as accompaniment to the right-hand melody. Most players find lifting some fingers while playing notes with others on the same hand difficult at first, but soon perfect the technique.

## Sustaining Pedal

Some piano composers indicate on the score when to use the sustaining pedal, but usually this is left to the performer. This pedal enriches the tone of the piano. Many of the effects demanded by nineteenth- and twentieth-century piano composers would be impossible without the sustaining pedal.

# Scarlatti
## 1685–1757

*Scarlatti was born in one of the most significant years in music history—the same year that the great composers Bach and George Frideric Handel were born. Scarlatti wrote 555 keyboard works, half of which were written during the last five years of his life.*

Domenico Scarlatti received his first music training from his father, Alessandro Scarlatti, who was also a composer. At the age of only sixteen Domenico was already a professional organist and composer at the Royal Court in Naples. By 1705 he had moved to Venice, where he studied while also making a living as a harpsichord player. Scarlatti then moved to Rome, where he wrote operas and church music and was harpsichord teacher to the exiled Queen Casimira of Poland.

With such a prestigious position, Scarlatti soon became well known as a teacher and performer as well as a composer. He was confident in his profession and particularly proud of his own keyboard technique. While living in Rome, he challenged Handel to a competition on the organ and harpsichord. Scarlatti was the victor on the harpsichord, and Handel on the organ! Later the two composers became firm friends.

The Music Lesson, *by the French painter Jean-Honoré Fragonard. Many of Scarlatti's keyboard compositions were written as teaching pieces for his pupils. As there was so little printed music in Scarlatti's day, it was usual for instrumental teachers to write their own.*

*The Venice of Scarlatti's day was a thriving city, where the cultural life was rich and varied. Through his work Scarlatti met many of the great artists and composers of his day, including Vivaldi.*

Most of Scarlatti's sonatas for keyboard emphasize some element of technique (which is why Scarlatti called them "exercises"). So one piece may demonstrate trills, another crossed hands, another scales, and so on.

One of the composer's most well-known pieces is the *Cat's Fugue* Sonata. This piece takes its name from the opening melody, which one critic said sounded like a cat jumping across the keys! Scarlatti's keyboard works have come down to us in their published form only, as the composer's original manuscripts have been lost.

In 1733 Scarlatti moved to Madrid, and from this time he composed mostly keyboard works. He became harpsichord teacher to Queen Barbara, who left him money and a valuable ring in her will. But Scarlatti never received her bequest, as he died a year before the queen.

*The first page of Scarlatti's* Esercizi per gravicembalo *(Exercises for Harpsichord).*

**ON THE CD**
**Track 1**
**Sonata in F minor**
**Allegro**

Today we call Domenico Scarlatti's harpsichord works sonatas, but Scarlatti called them *esercizi*—"exercises." Some sonatas are quite difficult to play, like this one, perhaps written for Scarlatti to perform at his own concerts, while others are much simpler and suitable as practice pieces for pupils.

Spanish Dancer, *by John Singer Sargent. Sometimes, by using repeated notes, Scarlatti gives the impression of clicking castanets. In other pieces the composer imitates the strumming of guitars.*

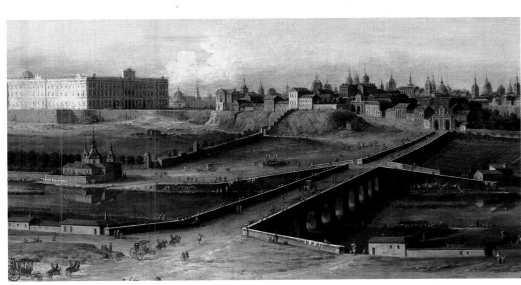

The Royal Palace in Madrid, *by Joli. Many of Scarlatti's keyboard sonatas were written here and dedicated to Queen Barbara.*

# Bach
## 1685–1750

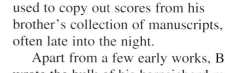

Johann Sebastian Bach received his first harpsichord and theory lessons from his brother, a professional organist and young Johann's guardian on the death of their parents. The nine-year-old boy was already interested in music and used to copy out scores from his brother's collection of manuscripts, often late into the night.

Apart from a few early works, Bach wrote the bulk of his harpsichord music in his later years. In 1722 he wrote what is probably his greatest work for keyboard—a collection of twenty-four preludes and fugues called *The Well-Tempered Clavier*. He wrote a second set of twenty-four in 1744. In Bach's day "clavier" simply meant "keyboard," and "tempered" meant "tuned."

Bach was the first major composer to write a keyboard concerto. The harpsichord at that time was generally used for accompanying other instruments, but Bach treated it as a solo instrument. He also wrote concertos for two, three, and even four harpsichords.

A strange story revolves around the composition of Bach's *Goldberg* Variations. The Russian ambassador to Dresden, Count Keyserlingk, suffered from insomnia, and regularly had his harpsichordist, Johann Goldberg, play for him before he retired to bed. The count commissioned a new work

*In Bach's day the piano was only in its infancy. Bach never specifically wrote music for piano—only the harpsichord— but today musicians often perform Bach on the piano.*

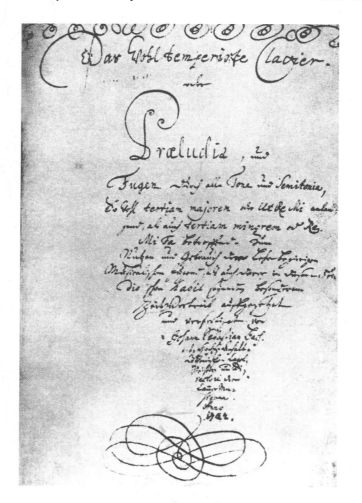

**Right:** *The title page of Bach's keyboard work* The Well-Tempered Clavier, *one of the greatest sets of keyboard pieces for study and performance ever written.*

from Bach to add to his collection of soothing pieces. Evidently Bach's piece suited the commission exactly, and the count presented him with a golden goblet filled with gold coins!

Bach often wrote pieces for his students to play. In 1720 his wife died, and the following year he married again. His second wife, Anna Magdalena, helped him with his work, mostly by copying out his music. He dedicated two books of keyboard pieces to her, intended for her own instruction as well as her enjoyment. Many of the pieces—as with all of Bach's keyboard works—are still used as instruction pieces today.

*Below: The imposing castle at Cöthen, where Bach was Kapellmeister (music director) to Prince Leopold. Taking up this position greatly upset his previous employer, the Duke of Saxe-Weimar, who kept Bach prisoner for almost a month to try and persuade him to stay!*

*Bach was a skilled performer on both the organ and harpsichord. In the course of his work he performed solo recital pieces as well as accompanying his own cantatas.*

**Below:** *Prince Leopold of Anhalt-Cöthen, Bach's employer from 1717 to 1723.*

## ON THE CD
### Tracks 2–4
### Italian *Concerto*
### I. *Allegro*  II. *Andante*  III. *Presto*

Bach wrote his *Italian* Concerto in 1735. It is for solo keyboard, which is unusual, as Bach's concertos usually have orchestral accompaniment. Bach gave the piece this title to indicate that it was written in an Italian style. The third and final movement, *Presto*, is one of the most rhythmically exciting of Bach's concerto movements.

# Mozart
## 1756–1791

*Mozart's first pieces for keyboard were published in 1763 when he was only seven years old.*

**Above:** *This picture of Leopold, Wolfgang, and Wolfgang's sister Nannerl was painted in 1780–81. In the background is a portrait of Mozart's mother, Maria Anna, who had died two years previously.*

**Left:** *King Louis XV of France. The Mozarts visited Paris in 1763, where they were invited to stay at the palace of Versailles for two weeks.*

Wolfgang Amadeus Mozart's father, Leopold, was himself a professional musician and composer. Wolfgang showed his musical gifts at a very early age by demanding to sit at the keyboard, where he could press the keys and listen to the sounds they made. At the earliest opportunity Mozart's father began lessons with his son, and by the age of four, we are told, Wolfgang could play his lessons perfectly.

Throughout his life Mozart was both performer and composer. In his early childhood the harpsichord was the most fashionable keyboard instrument, but by the end of the eighteenth century

*This famous picture by the French artist, Michel Barthelemy Ollivier, painted in 1766, shows Mozart at the wealthy Prince de Conti's palace playing for an audience of French nobility.*

*The Archbishop of Salzburg, Mozart's employer. As violinist and composer to the archbishop, Mozart was extremely unhappy. The archbishop had little time for music, and treated Mozart like an unskilled servant.*

the piano had replaced it. All of Mozart's later keyboard works were written for the piano. Mozart's skill as a keyboard player served him well throughout his life. As a performer, not only did he earn a living from his playing, but by playing his own works, he could advertise his ability as a composer and so encourage the more wealthy of his listeners to commission works from him.

In 1773 Mozart wrote his first piano concerto, and from this date he wrote piano concertos to the end of his life. When, in 1781 after moving to Vienna, he was dismissed by his employer, the Archbishop of Salzburg, he threw himself into a fury of composing piano concertos to perform at his own concerts. Within four years he had written fifteen new works. These pieces are among the composer's greatest achievements.

Mozart's first important keyboard sonatas were written in 1774. He called them clavier sonatas, indicating that the music could be played on the piano or the harpsichord. Most of these works were written in the early part of Mozart's life; we have very few keyboard sonatas from the composer's mature years.

### ON THE CD
### Tracks 5–16
### 12 Variations on "Ah, vous dirai-je, maman"

Mozart wrote this well-known set of piano variations in 1778. The variations begin with the main tune, or theme, a French melody that we know as "Twinkle, Twinkle, Little Star." The tune is followed by twelve variations.

# Beethoven
## 1770–1827

*For the first thirty years of his life Beethoven was known as a pianist rather than a composer. He performed at public concerts as well as in the houses of the Viennese nobility, often playing his own compositions.*

Ludwig van Beethoven received his first keyboard lessons from his father. The five-year-old Ludwig made astounding progress, and at the age of seven he played before the court at Bonn, Germany. Later, Beethoven took lessons from the court organist Christian Gottlob Neefe, who arranged for one of the twelve-year-old Beethoven's compositions—a set of variations on a march tune—to be published. This was the composer's earliest piano piece to appear in print.

In 1792 Beethoven moved to Vienna, where he lived for the rest of his life. In 1795 he performed a newly completed piano concerto. The concert was a great success, and one Viennese critic called Beethoven "a giant among pianoforte players." Beethoven was soon in great demand as a performer and piano teacher in the houses of the rich.

As well as large-scale works—concertos and sonatas—Beethoven also wrote smaller works for piano, often to use as teaching pieces. His famous Minuet in G is still popular today with beginner pianists. Another piece, equally popular, is "Für Elise." For many years pianists wondered who Elise was, but

**Above:** *Bonn in the late eighteenth century. When Beethoven's father took young Ludwig to play before the court at Bonn, he removed two years from the boy's age to make his playing seem more impressive!*

**Left:** *Christian Gottlob Neefe (1748–1798) taught Beethoven piano and composition. In 1783 he said that the thirteen-year-old Beethoven "would surely become a second Wolfgang Amadeus Mozart were he to continue as he has begun."*

now the mystery may be solved. It is thought the music was intended for a young pupil called Therese, but an incompetent copyist mistakenly wrote Elise on the title page of the music!

In all, Beethoven wrote five piano concertos and a concerto for piano, violin, and cello. He also wrote much chamber music for piano and other instruments, including sonatas, trios, quartets, and a quintet. In many of these compositions the piano takes the lead; in every Beethoven work in which it appears, the instrument is treated with great reverence and sensitivity.

*Baden-Baden, where Beethoven went in 1810 hoping to find a cure for his deafness. Throughout his life Beethoven visited many doctors to try and find cures for his various ailments. After 1822 he became resigned to his deafness and sought no further cures.*

**ON THE CD**
**Track 18**
**Piano Sonata No. 14**
**in C-sharp minor (Moonlight)**

Beethoven composed this sonata in 1801. The name *Moonlight* was given to it by the Viennese poet Heinrich Rellstab, who said the first movement reminded him of moonlight flickering on the ripples of Lake Lucerne, in Switzerland.

Night Seaport, *by Claude Joseph Vernet, 1771.*

*To Beethoven, the piano was the most important of all the instruments. Although after 1808, because of his increasing deafness, he had to give up most of his performing work, the keyboard still played a major part in his compositions.*

# Schubert
## 1797–1828

Though Franz Peter Schubert was a competent pianist, he wrote no piano concertos, but he has left us with fifteen piano sonatas. His final three sonatas were written when he was already seriously ill, just two months before his death. Schubert also wrote works for piano duet. One of his greatest works in this form is the Grand Duo in C major, which some music historians think may have first been a sketch for a symphony.

*Schubert composed his first piano pieces when he was a chorister in Vienna. Sadly, few works from this period survive today. Still with us, however, is his Fantasy for piano duet. Schubert was only thirteen when he wrote this piece, which marked the start of his career as a great piano composer.*

***Right:*** *Schubertiade, 1821, by the artist Leopold Kupelweiser. Through their regular evening concerts Schubert's friends made great efforts to publicize his music. Here, Schubert is seated at the piano.*

Some of Schubert's happiest times were spent enjoying musical evenings at the homes of his friends. Often much of the music performed at these gatherings was by Schubert. His friends nicknamed these concerts "Schubertiades," and Schubert would usually be pianist for the evening. For these and similar occasions he wrote many sets of piano waltzes and much dance music, including two sets of waltzes called *Valses nobles* and *Valses sentimentales*. These pieces combine different waltz tunes, and may have inspired Johann Strauss to write his own extremely popular waltzes.

Much of Schubert's chamber music includes the piano, and, like Beethoven, he always gave the instrument an important place in the music. Schubert was one of the first composers to write for piano and string quartet, and compositions like his *Trout Quintet* are much loved by concert-goers. In the slow movement of this piece Schubert uses a melody from his

song "The Trout." It was quite common for Schubert to use melodies from his songs in instrumental works. In his great piano work the *Wanderer Fantasy* he uses material from his song "The Wanderer." Schubert wrote several other fantasies for piano. A fantasy means the music is less formal— more relaxed and carefree.

*Zseliz Castle, summer home of the wealthy Esterházy family, where Schubert taught the two daughters of the count. During the peaceful summer spent at the castle in 1818, Schubert composed piano duets for the sisters to play.*

**Left:** *The Stadtkonvikt in Vienna, the school where Schubert studied from ages eleven to sixteen and wrote his first piano compositions. The director of the school, Innocenz Lang, said Schubert had "a musical talent."*

**Right:** *The title page for eight variations for piano duet dedicated to Beethoven "by his admirer and worshiper, Franz Schubert." Although he idolized Beethoven, this is the only work Schubert dedicated to him.*

# Chopin
## 1810–1849

Chopin belonged to a time in Europe when nationalism was very important, and composers, writers, and artists expressed their nationalistic feelings through their art. Chopin's homeland was Poland, and we see him reinforcing this connection in compositions that incorporate the dance forms and rhythms of his native country.

Warsaw, Chopin's birthplace. At the age of only nine he was invited to take part in a public charity concert. Chopin played a piano concerto, and the concert was a great success.

***Right:***
*Village merrymaking in Poland.*

Frédéric Chopin began studying piano in 1817, at age seven, and almost immediately was tapping out his own tunes at the keyboard. That same year, his first composition was published—a Polish dance called a "polonaise"—and the following year he played in a public concert in Warsaw. In his early teens Chopin played before the Tsar of Russia, who presented him with a diamond ring. In later years, when living abroad, Chopin wrote more dance music that reminded him so much of his own country.

When he was twenty-one, Chopin moved to Paris, where he performed, taught, and composed for the piano. He became well known as a piano teacher, and earned large sums of money performing at fashionable soirées held at the magnificent houses of wealthy Parisians. Though living in France, Chopin was still passionate about his native country: he wrote fourteen more polonaises and thirty-one mazurkas (another popular Polish dance). Sometimes Chopin based his compositions on unusual scales taken from Gypsy music, which gave these compositions a folk-music flavor.

Chopin wrote few really large compositions and very little music with orchestra. Yet his two piano concertos, composed between the years 1829 and 1830, were an amazing

*Chopin performing at Posen, Poland. As a pianist Chopin was largely self-taught. He used techniques that were considered eccentric then, but that modern pianists would consider essential to good playing.*

*The waltz swept through Europe in the first half of the nineteenth century, although some sections of polite society disapproved, as it allowed men and women to dance too closely!*

feat for an inexperienced composer of barely twenty. The works were performed in Warsaw in 1830 with Chopin himself at the keyboard. After this, Chopin wrote no more piano concertos, concentrating instead on smaller works for solo piano, such as the Preludes and Nocturnes. "Nocturne" means "evening piece," but in music the word is used to describe a quiet, gentle composition. Some of Chopin's nocturnes are his most famous works.

Chopin called one set of compositions Études, a French word meaning "studies." The *Revolutionary* Étude is one of the most popular pieces in this collection. It is said that when Chopin heard that his native Warsaw had been captured by the Russians, he expressed his anger in the fiery music of this work.

Chopin's Waltzes have always remained particularly popular. They are, however, not for dancing but for the enjoyment of pianists and concert audiences. It is sometimes thought that the *Minute* Waltz was given this name because it takes a minute to play. But this is a mistake. The title is French, not English, and means "Little Waltz." To play it in a minute would be far too fast!

Toward the end of his life Chopin was seriously ill with tuberculosis, and in the three years before he died, he wrote almost nothing. But in 1849 he wrote two mazurkas, which, as it turned out, were to be his last works. He died before he was even able to try the pieces out on the piano.

**ON THE CD**
**Track 20**
**Polonaise No. 6 in A flat**
**(Heroic)**

This polonaise, one of twelve written by Chopin, was composed in 1836. The powerful, "heroic" nature of the music prompted the popular name (which is not by Chopin) of this work.

# Schumann
## 1810–1856

From an early age Robert Schumann showed himself to be extremely musical, yet his parents were determined he should become a lawyer. He entered university to study law, but soon abandoned his legal studies to take up music. He immediately began an intense period of study, setting his sights on becoming Europe's finest piano virtuoso. But at the age of twenty-two a personal disaster destroyed all his concert hall ambitions. Schumann had been using a mechanical device he made himself to strengthen the fourth finger of his right hand, with the result that he permanently damaged that hand. This led him to concentrate all his energies on composition. He had composed since he was a child, so this idea was not new to him. He took composition lessons, and soon began to produce his first pieces.

Schumann's first published work was a set of variations for piano, the *Abegg* Variations, named after his friend Meta Abegg. The composer cleverly used the musical letters in his friend's name—A, B, E, G, G,—as the basis of the main theme of the music. Two years later he wrote his first collection of piano pieces, which were to set the style of his mature works. He gave the pieces the title *Papillons* (Butterflies)— probably to describe the light, airy nature of the music.

Like many artists, Schumann's moods changed quickly and frequently. One day his wife, Clara, jokingly told him that he reminded her of a child. This comment suggested to Schumann the idea of writing a suite of "childhood" pieces. The result was *Kinderscenen* (Scenes from Childhood). The most popular piece in the set is "Traümerei," whose music is slow and reflective and aptly suited to its title (Dreaming). Schumann later wrote a set of pieces for

*Although Schumann wrote orchestral music, chamber music, and choral works—including an opera—he was always more at ease writing piano music.*

**Left:** *Schumann and his wife, Clara. Clara was a brilliant concert pianist who achieved enormous success as a touring virtuoso playing a variety of music, including works by her husband. Schumann wrote his Piano Concerto for her.*

In his piano work
Carnaval, *Schumann's aim
is to portray a carnival
scene in music. All the
pieces have titles, several
of them using the names of
traditional carnival
characters. Other
movements describe
himself and Clara.*

children to play, called *Album für die Jugend* (Album for the Young).

In 1835 Schumann composed his famous *Carnaval*. Several pieces in the work suggest carnival scenes and fairground characters, but Schumann probably chose the title simply to suggest the carefree and holiday feel of the music.

Schumann wrote only one piano concerto. The piece began life in 1841 as a single movement entitled "Fantasy." Clara, who was herself a pianist, gave the first performance of the piece. Four years later Schumann decided to expand the movement into a full-length concerto. This new work was a great success—a welcome relief for Schumann during a time of increasing unhappiness caused by the onset of illness.

*Spavento*

*Trivelino*

**ON THE CD**
**Track 21**
**Fantasiestücke**
*II: "Aufschwung" (Soaring)*

Schumann wrote this collection of eight pieces in 1837. As with much of his piano music, Schumann wrote the titles of the pieces only after he had written the music: "Soaring" is stormy music reflecting Schumann's ambitious and passionate character.

**Left:** *Spavento and Trivelino,
traditional characters from
Italian theater. Schumann was
always attracted by
pantomime and the theater.*

# Liszt
## 1811–1886

As a pianist at the height of his success, and the first of the great piano recitalists, Liszt was virtually unrivaled. His playing influenced pianists in his own time and those who followed him. Some of the composer's pieces represent some of the most difficult piano music ever written.

**Right:** Liszt playing for the Viennese imperial family. The floral decorations show the high esteem in which the pianist was held.

Franz Liszt began piano lessons with his father at the age of six, and by the age of nine he was already playing in public. In 1823 his father took him to Vienna, where the talented twelve-year-old gave a highly successful concert, impressing the great Beethoven, who was in the audience. Liszt gave further concerts in France, Switzerland, and England before finally settling in Paris.

Liszt wrote two piano concertos. When the first was played in Vienna, it was not a success and was severely criticized by the music critic Eduard Hanslick—especially the use of a solo triangle in the third movement. Hanslick sarcastically called the work "the triangle concerto." Liszt had to wait twelve years to hear his work performed in Vienna again. This time, however, the piece was a great success.

Liszt preferred to write descriptive and display piano music rather than more formal pieces. However, one formal piece, his Sonata for the piano, is now considered one of his greatest works. Liszt dedicated the sonata to Schumann in return for an earlier dedication made by Schumann to Liszt.

In 1850 Liszt wrote what is now probably his most well-known piano composition. It is the second piece in a set of three compositions, each one called "Liebestraum" (Love's Dream). Each piece is based on one of Liszt's own songs.

**Above:** *A portrait of Liszt in Hungarian national costume. Liszt was born a Hungarian and he was proud of his background. He spent years researching the folk music of his own country. He used these melodies, rhythms, and dance styles in his compositions, particularly the Hungarian Rhapsodies.*

**Right:** *The composer Richard Wagner and Liszt. The two composers were great friends, each supporting the other in their music. In 1870 Wagner married Liszt's daughter Cosima.*

**Above:** *The music critic Eduard Hanslick (1825–1904). Hanslick was an extremely influential man, passionately against the new "Romantic" style of music, which composers such as Liszt and Wagner were writing.*

**ON THE CD**
**Track 22**
**"Mazeppa,"**
**Transcendental *Étude* No. 4**

Liszt was fascinated by the story of Mazeppa, who, an outcast from his own land, endured terrible torture before finally rising up to be leader of the Cossacks. Liszt wrote several works based on this theme.

# Brahms
## 1833–1897

*In the Germany of Brahms's day composers were divided into two schools. One school, which included the great opera composer Wagner, wrote in the Romantic style. Brahms, however, belonged to the Classical school that followed directly from Beethoven. For this reason he suffered greatly from some critics, who dubbed him "old-fashioned."*

***Right:** An announcement of a soirée with Brahms, the violinist and conductor Joachim, and Clara Schumann. Brahms met Joachim in 1853 and through him met the Schumanns.*

Johannes Brahms's father was a double bass player in a local orchestra in Hamburg, Germany, and it was from him that Johannes received his first music instruction. At a public concert given when he was only fourteen, the young composer played his own set of piano variations, based on a folk song. Throughout Brahms's childhood, his

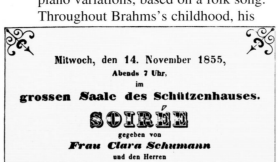

Mitwoch, den 14. November 1855,
Abends 7 Uhr,
im
grossen Saale des Schützenhauses.
SOIRÉE
gegeben von
*Frau Clara Schumann*
und den Herren
*Joseph Joachim* und *Johannes Brahms.*

PROGRAMM.

Erster Theil.

1. Sonate von Mozart in Adur für Clavier und Violine, gespielt von Clara Schumann und Joseph Joachim.
2. Fantaisie (op. 77.) von Beethoven, gespielt von Johannes Brahms.
3. Chaconne von Johann Sebastian Bach für Violine allein, gespielt von Joseph Joachim.

Zweiter Theil.

4. Symphonische Etuden (Etudes en forme de Variations) von Robert Schumann, gespielt von Clara Schumann.
5. Sonate Gdur für Clavier und Violine von Joseph Haydn, gespielt von Johannes Brahms und Joseph Joachim.
6. a. Sarabande und Gavotte für Clavier von Johannes Brahms, b. Marsch von Fr. Schubert, gespielt von Johannes Brahms.
7. Caprice und Variationen für Violine von Paganini, gespielt von Joseph Joachim.

Billets à 1 rtl. sind in der Buch- und Musikalien-Handlung von **F. A. Weber**, Langgasse 78., zu haben. An der Kasse kostet das Billet 1 rtl. 10 sgr.

Wedel'sche Hofbuchdruckerei.

family was extremely poor, and when he left school, he had to earn what money he could playing the piano in the seedy taverns and dancing saloons of the Hamburg docks area.

Yet the young composer always found time to write music. While still in his late teens he composed three piano sonatas. At this time he met Schumann, who gave him great encouragement and helped him find a publisher for the works.

Brahms's first piano concerto was also his first large-scale composition. The music began life as a piano sonata for four hands (two players playing on one piano). It was when the work was newly completed that a musical friend suggested Brahms rewrite it as a concerto, which he did. At the first public performance, in Hanover in 1859, Brahms was the soloist, and Brahms's good friend the violinist Joachim conducted. Unfortunately the concert was a terrible failure—some of the audience even hissed. After this Brahms did not write another piano concerto for over twenty years.

Brahms wrote solo piano works throughout his composing life. He wrote the four Ballades when he was only twenty-one. These powerful Romantic pieces were Brahms's first mature works for piano. Ten years later he wrote a set of Waltzes, inspired by

**Right:** *Scene near Bad Ischl, Brahms's favorite holiday resort. He always took work with him on holidays, although he left at least part of each day for walking and socializing.*

Schubert. Some of these pieces show Brahms's love of folk and Gypsy music, as do the *Hungarian* Dances, written in 1869 and 1880.

Brahms wrote piano pieces in many of the forms made popular by his predecessors. The word "ballade" was first used by Chopin. But the title "Capriccio," which Brahms used to describe a short piano piece that was light and whimsical, was his own. He wrote seven compositions in this style. He also wrote eighteen Intermezzos—pieces that are much slower and more Romantic.

**Left:** *Harvest festival celebrations in Hungary by the painter Agost Canzi. When the* Hungarian *Dances were first published, Brahms was careful to make it clear that they were only arrangements of folk music and not original compositions, but some of his critics still accused him of passing off traditional music as his own.*

# Debussy
## 1862–1918

Claude Debussy was nine years old when he began playing the piano, receiving free lessons from a local amateur pianist. But by the time Debussy was sixteen, his goal of becoming a pianist was less important to him. Now he enjoyed improvising at the piano, moving strange chords one after the other up or down the scale, and using unpredictable harmonies.

As a composer, Debussy's first love was always the piano, although he was well into his twenties before his first piano works began to appear. In 1888 he wrote the earliest piano pieces that are still played regularly today—the two *Arabesques*. The pieces are inspired by the word "arabesque" (meaning "decoration") and contain some elaborate piano writing. Two years later Debussy wrote one of his most famous

pieces—"Clair de lune" (Moonlight). This gentle, quiet piece is similar in atmosphere to the opening movement of Beethoven's *Moonlight* Sonata.

Debussy often gave his works unusual and nonmusical titles. He called a set of three descriptive pieces

*Above: The Paris Exhibition of 1889, where Debussy was particularly impressed with the playing of the Indonesian gamelan orchestra—a body of musicians performing on gongs, metallophones, xylophones, strings, wind instruments, and drums. His "Pagodas" was inspired by gamelan music.*

*Debussy entered the Paris Conservatoire of Music at the age of only eleven. His compositions were from the start unusual, and he irritated several of his tutors because he wouldn't respect the "rules" when doing the music exercises they gave him.*

***Below:** Debussy captured the atmosphere of the ancient city in his piano piece "An Evening Scene in Granada."*

published in 1903 *Estampes* (Engravings in Music). The pictures Debussy describes in the music are "Pagodas," "An Evening Scene in Granada," and "Gardens in the Rain."

In 1908 Debussy wrote his piano suite *Children's Corner*, dedicated to his daughter Claude-Emma. The six titles in the set portray a child's images. The music is simpler than most piano music by Debussy, although still too difficult for anyone but an adult or gifted child to play.

When pianists think of Debussy, they probably first think of his two books of Preludes. The word "prelude" usually means an introductory piece. But in music, composers often use it to describe a single composition—as Debussy did. Many of the Preludes, such as "The Girl with the Flaxen Hair" and "The Submerged Cathedral," are now favorite pieces on the concert platform.

In 1915 Debussy embarked on writing a collection of piano Études (studies). The pieces are divided into two books. In Book 1 Debussy concentrates on piano fingering, and in Book 2 on how to produce the best tone (sound) from the piano. Each study demonstrates a particular piano technique: playing octaves, repeated notes, arpeggios, and so on. Debussy dedicated the music to the memory of Chopin, who himself had offered so much to advance piano technique.

*Left:* This photograph of Debussy was taken in 1905, at the time he was writing some of his most successful music. Although at the peak of his composing life, he had little more than ten years to live.

*Nadezhda von Meck, wealthy Russian patron of Pyotr Il'yich Tchaikovsky, employed Debussy as pianist in her small orchestra. This was Debussy's first paid appointment after leaving the Paris Conservatoire.*

**ON THE CD**
**Track 24**
**L'Isle joyeuse**

Debussy wrote this work when he was forty-two, at a time when he was composing some of his most well-known works for the piano. The piece is one of Debussy's most colorful, and exploits the full tonal range of the instrument.

# Great Players

## JOHANN HUMMEL
### 1778–1837

The Austrian composer and pianist Johann Hummel was a child prodigy on the keyboard. Between the ages of eight and ten he studied with Mozart in Vienna. When he was eleven, his father took him on a concert tour of Germany, Holland, and England, where he met Franz Joseph Haydn, from whom he later took lessons. Hummel toured regularly, although he still found time to write an important book on piano teaching and compose much extremely attractive music—including seven piano concertos. Hummel's playing is said to have been light, precise, and delicate.

## SIGISMOND THALBERG
### 1812–1871

Sigismond Thalberg was a pupil of Hummel. In his middle years he rose to be the greatest pianist of his day, and at one time, while living in Paris, he was a rival of the great Liszt himself. At his concerts he mostly played his own music, which he wrote specifically to show off the capabilities of the piano as well as his own exceptional keyboard skills. Thalberg's playing style was admired for its great expression as much as for its dazzling technique.

## ANTON RUBINSTEIN
### 1829–1894

Anton Rubinstein was born in Russia, and from a child virtuoso (he performed in Paris at the age of ten), he grew to be one of the greatest pianists of the nineteenth century. His career also included conducting, teaching, and composing—he wrote five piano concertos. Rubinstein performed from memory—highly unusual at the time—and a feat that earned him considerable acclaim. His playing was considered second only to that of Liszt, who had encouraged Rubinstein as a child.

# Great Players

## HANS VON BÜLOW
## 1830–1894

The German conductor and pianist Hans von Bülow studied under the famous Liszt, and later married Liszt's daughter. His first concert tour, in 1853 at the age of twenty-three, took him to his native Germany and also to Austria. In later years he encouraged and performed the works of Brahms, and in 1875 he gave the premiere of Tchaikovsky's First Piano Concerto. As a pianist, he was remarkable for his impressive memory and wide repertoire.

## CARL TAUSIG
## 1841–1871

The Polish pianist Carl Tausig died of typhoid at the young age of twenty-nine, yet he remains one of the most respected and famous virtuoso pianists of his generation. His teachers included Thalberg and Liszt. At seventeen he gave a highly successful concert in Berlin, conducted by the youthful Hans von Bülow. As a pianist, Tausig was known for his breathtaking technique, but most of all his amazing memory —he was said to be able to play the entire classical repertoire from memory.

## FERRUCCIO BUSONI
## 1866–1924

Ferruccio Busoni was born an Italian but spent most of his life in Germany. He gave his first solo performance in Vienna at the age of eight. At the age of sixteen his gifted piano playing and his first compositions gained him admittance to the Accadèmia Filarmònica, a highly respected music society in Bologna, Italy, as the youngest member since Mozart. Busoni's most famous pupil was the Australian composer and pianist Percy Grainger.

# Great Players

## SERGEI RACHMANINOV
## 1873–1943

When Sergei Rachmaninov graduated in 1892 from the Moscow Conservatory it was with distinction—as both a pianist and composer. As a composer, Rachmaninov wrote a considerable number of piano works, including the highly popular Second Piano Concerto, written in 1901. After the 1917 Revolution Rachmaninov moved from Russia to Switzerland. From 1921 he lived in the U.S.A., while continuing his flourishing worldwide concert career. As a pianist, Rachmaninov was fortunate in having an unusually wide hand span.

## ARTUR RUBINSTEIN
## 1887–1982

At the age of eight the Polish-born pianist Artur Rubinstein gave his first public performance, playing a Mozart piano concerto. In 1900 at the age of only thirteen he made his Berlin debut. As a student, he studied with the legendary Polish pianist Ignacy Paderewski. Rubinstein gave regular piano recitals until his retirement at the age of eighty-nine. His finest performances are most often associated with the music of the greatest nineteenth-century composers—Beethoven, Schubert, Schumann, Chopin, and Brahms.

## SOLOMON
## 1902–1988

In his professional career the British pianist Solomon Cutner was always known only by his first name—Solomon. From an early age he was an outstanding pianist, performing Tchaikovsky's First Piano Concerto at the age of eight at the famous Queen's Hall in London. At the age of fourteen he became a pupil of Mathilde Verne, who herself had studied with Clara Schumann, Robert Schumann's wife. As a pianist, Solomon was particularly known for his performances of Mozart, as well as music of the great nineteenth-century piano composers.

# Great Players

## VLADIMIR HOROWITZ
## 1904–1989

Vladimir Horowitz was born in Kiev, Russia. He first appeared on the concert platform in 1922 in his native Russia, and from then on rapidly acquired an international reputation. He was particularly known for his performances of Liszt and other nineteenth-century Romantic composers. In 1986, at the age of eighty-two, he returned to Russia after an absence of many years to give his final performance.

## SVYATOSLAV RICHTER
## born 1915

The Russian pianist Svyatoslav Richter studied at the Moscow Conservatory and later became one of his country's most outstanding musicians, winning the much-coveted Stalin Prize in 1949. In the early part of his career he became associated with the piano music of Prokofiev. He played in England in 1950, and from this time began his association with Benjamin Britten and the Aldeburgh Festival. As a pianist, he is extremely self-critical, which has led him on occasion to cancel concerts at short notice.

## MICHELANGELI
## 1920–1995

Arturo Benedetti Michelangeli was professionally known only by the second half of his surname. He studied at the Milan Conservatory, and in 1939 he won the Geneva International Piano Competition, which started him off on an international career. Throughout his life Michelangeli was prone to sporadic illness, which restricted him and caused him often to cancel concerts. As well as a performer, Michelangeli was also a teacher of international repute.

# CD Track Listings

**Figures in [...] identify the track numbers from the EMI recording.**
**Track lengths are listed in minutes and seconds.**

**EMI** is one of the world's leading classical music companies, with a rich heritage and reputation for producing great and often definitive recordings performed by the world's greatest artists. As a result of this long and accomplished recording history, EMI has an exceptional catalog of classical recordings, exceptional in both quality and quantity. It is from this catalog that EMI has selected the recordings detailed in the track listing below. Many of the recordings featured are available on CD and cassette from EMI.

Domenico Scarlatti 1685–1757
[1]  **Sonata in F minor** Allegro K183 (L473)                     5.25
Christian Zacharias (piano) ℗1985+

Johann Sebastian Bach 1685–1750
**Italian Concerto** BWV971
[2]  I: Allegro                                                     3.45
[3]  II: Andante                                                    4.43
[4]  III: Presto                                                    3.19
Stanislav Bunin (piano) ℗1990†

Wolfgang Amadeus Mozart 1756–1791
**12 Variations on "Ah, vous dirai-je, maman"** K265

| | | | |
|---|---|---|---|
| [5] Theme | 0.48 | [6] Variation I | 0.42 |
| [7] Variation II | 0.44 | [8] Variation III | 0.44 |
| [9] Variation IV | 0.42 | [10] Variation V | 0.46 |
| [11] Variation VI | 0.41 | [12] Variation VII | 0.43 |
| [13] Variation VIII | 0.51 | [14] Variation IX | 0.42 |
| [15] Variation X | 0.41 | [16] Variation XI | 2.25 |
| [17] Variation XII | 1.16 | | |

Alexander Lonquich (piano) ℗1991+

Ludwig van Beethoven 1770–1827
**Piano Sonata No. 14 in C-sharp minor**
Op. 27 No. 2 (*Moonlight*)
[18]  I: Adagio sostenuto                                          5.49
Dame Moura Lympany (piano) ℗1991

Franz Schubert 1797–1828
[19]  **Impromptu in A flat** Op. 90 No. 4                          7.14
Daniel Adni (piano) ℗1975/DRM 1988*

Frédéric Chopin 1810–1849
[20]  **Polonaise No. 6 in A flat** Op. 53 (*Heroic*)              6.57
Maurizio Pollini (piano) ℗1970/1992*

Robert Schumann 1810–1856
[21]  **Fantasiestücke** Op. 12—II: "Aufschwung" (*Soaring*) 3.35
Sylvia Kersenbaum (piano) ℗1975/1995*#

Franz Liszt 1811–1886
[22]  **"Mazeppa"** *Transcendental* Étude No. 4                    7.42
Tzimon Barto (piano) ℗1989

Johannes Brahms 1833–1897
[23]  **Rhapsody in G minor** Op. 79 No. 2                          6.25
Garrick Ohlsson (piano) ℗1978/1995*

Claude Debussy 1862–1918
[24]  *L'Isle joyeuse*                                              5.51
Daniel Adni (piano) ℗1972/1989*

73.14

[DDD/*ADD]

# Acknowledgments

The publisher would like to thank the following for their permission to use illustrative material reproduced in this book:

*a= above, b=below, c=center, r=right, l=left*

**AKG, London**: 15, 22*l*, 22*r*, 24*al*, 26*a*, 26*b*, 27*r*, 28*c*, 31*l*, 32*l*, 34*r*, 34*b*, 36*a*, 39*c*, 40*al*, 41*l*, 43*l*. **Bridgeman Art Library**: 6*l* (St James's Church, Piccadilly, London), 6*b* (Fenton House), 7*a* (Fenton House), 23*l* (Index/Royal Palace, Naples), 23*r* (private collection), 25*r* (Heimatmuseum, Köthen), 26*r* (Mozartmuseum, Salzburg), 27*l* (Giraudon/Chateau de Versailles), 35*a* (Giraudon/Louvres, Paris), 35*l* & *r* (Casa Goldoni, Venice), 37*b* (private collection), 38*a* (Historisches Museum der Stadt, Vienna), 40*b* (Christie's, London), 40*r* (private collection). **E.T. Archive**: 28*a*, 29*l*, 30*r*, 31*a*, 34*al*, 36*b*, 39*b*. Lebrecht Collection: 6*ar*, 13*a*, 23*a*, 24*b*, 25*l*, 25*c*, 28*b*, 29*a*, 29*r*, 30*l*, 31*br*, 32*c*, 32*b*, 33*l*, 33*r*, 37*al*, 37*ar*, 38*c*, 41*r*, 42*l*, *r*, *c*, 43*c* & *l*, 44*r*, 45*r*. The **Metropolitan Museum of Art**, The Crosby Brown Collection of Musical Instruments, 1889, 12*al*. **Orbis Publishing Ltd**: 8*l*. **Performing Arts Library**/Clive Barda: 7*b* (Colin Willoughby), 8*r*, 9*b*, 10*a*, 10*bl*, 10*ar*, 11*a*, 11*b* (Royal Philharmonic Orchestra), 44*c*, 45*l* & *c*. **Pictorial Press**: 11*r*. **Redferns**: 9*a* (David Redfern). **Telegraph Colour Library** (panels): 1*r*, 3*r*, 12*l*, 15*r*, 47*r*. **Victoria & Albert Museum**: 13*b*.

Front cover photograph by Michael Banks (and panel photographs used on pages 4, 5). Back cover: Cristofori's piano: The Metropolitan Museum of Art, The Crosby Brown Collection of Musical Instruments, 1889; portrait of Chopin: AKG, London. Front flap and back cover keyboard: Telegraph Colour Library.

Photographs on pages 16–21 by Phil Rudge. Endpapers: score from Beethoven's Concerto No. 5 ('Emperor') reproduced with permission from Eulenberg Editions Ltd.

The publishers are also grateful to: EMI Records UK for their cooperation and expertise in compiling and producing the CD. Bösendorfer London Piano Centre for photographs reproduced on pages 16–21, and also the "action" featured on the back cover. Stephen Carroll Turner for photographs reproduced on page 18. Harry Lloyd for photographs used on pages 20–21.

# Index

all musical works appear in italics